The burglar got in through the bathroom, somehow.

Probably up through the loo. Chuck didn't trust that loo. The bath was friendly, but the loo made coming-to-get-you noises, though Danielle and her mum were always careful to shut the door before it made them, so that it couldn't come rushing round the flat after Chuck, like the vacuum cleaner.

Anyway, she heard a click and a rattle. Footsteps! A person.

The bathroom door! The person was letting the loo out!

No, not yet. Footsteps in the hallway.

Coming to the living-room door.

Chuck bolted . . .

Also available by Peter Dickinson, and published by Doubleday/Corgi Books:

TIME AND THE CLOCK MICE, ETCETERA

For older readers:

EVA

A.K.

TULKU

A BONE FROM A DRY SEA

SHADOW OF A HERO

PETER DICKINSON

Chuck and Danielle

Illustrated by Robin Lawrie

CORGI YEARLING BOOKS

CHUCK AND DANIELLE
A CORGI YEARLING BOOK: 0 440 863554

First published in Great Britain by Doubleday,
a division of Transworld Publishers Ltd

PRINTING HISTORY
Doubleday edition published 1966
Corgi Yearling edition published 1998
3 5 7 9 10 8 6 4 2

Corgi Yearling Books are published by Transworld Publishers Ltd,
62-63 Uxbridge Road, Ealing, London W5 5SA.
in Australia by Transworld Publishers, c/o Random House Australia Pty Ltd,
20 Alfred Street, Milsons Point, NSW 2061,
in New Zealand by Transworld Publishers, c/o Random House New Zealand,
18 Poland Road, Glenfield, Auckland, and
in South Africa by Transworld Publishers, c/o Random House (Pty) Ltd,
Endulini, 5a Jubilee Road, Parktown 2193.

Made and printed in Great Britain by
Mackays of Chatham PLC, Chatham, Kent

for
ROWAN, HOLLY
and
HAZEL
(a.k.a. 'Chuck')

CONTENTS

Chuck Saves the Universe

Chuck is a whippet.

She looks like a small greyhound, fawn-coloured, with a white band round her neck and white front feet. She is small, even for a whippet, because she was the runt of her litter. Her real name is Golden Hazelwood Mungo Paternoster, because she is very well-bred, but she belongs to Danielle, who isn't bothered about being well-bred. Danielle calls her Chuck. She was a present from Danielle's Uncle Ron, who is an oil engineer.

Danielle lives with her mum in a flat at the

bottom of an old house in a large town in the middle of England. There's just Danielle and her mum.

And Chuck.

People say whippets are nervous dogs, especially the well-bred ones.

Chuck isn't nervous.

She isn't *just* nervous.

She's scared.

Everything is coming to get her.

Paper bags are coming to get her, blowing along the pavement.

Pigeons are coming to get her, whooshing down for crumbs.

Supermarket trolleys are coming to get her, just standing there, not doing anything. (But they *might*, any moment.)

Motorcycles – of course they're coming to get her.

Podge is coming to get her.

Podge?

Podge is Jenny's old bear. Jenny is Danielle's best friend, and Podge is the old bear which used to be a new bear when Jenny's gran gave him to Jenny's mum years and years and years ago. Once, when Chuck was a puppy, Jenny made Podge growl at her, and since then Chuck has just *known* that Podge is coming to get her.

When something comes to get Chuck she bolts to the end of her lead. If anyone's in the way, she bolts between their legs and trips them up. Sometimes they land on Chuck, which as far as she can see proves she was right. Something *was* coming to get her.

Danielle's mum is a lab technician at the hospital, doing tests for meningitis and things like that. She works the early shift so that she can get home and do the shopping and so on and still be there when

Danielle gets back from school. Sometimes she takes Chuck with her when she goes out.

'That dog's a menace,' she said one day.

'What happened?' said Danielle.

'Fool of a man dropped a coin,' said her mum.

'A coin?' said Danielle.

This was a new one. It seemed a bit wimpish, even for Chuck.

'Well, people were stamping around trying to stop it rolling,' said her mum.

'That would do it,' said Danielle. 'So she got between your legs?'

'Not mine,' said her mum. 'That wouldn't have been so bad. I'm going to give her away.'

'No!' said Danielle, though she was pretty sure it was only a joke.

'To someone who lives on a desert island,' said her mum.

'There'd be gulls coming to get her,' said Danielle. 'And waves. And coconuts. Anyway, it's our duty to keep her. One day Chuck's going to save the universe.'

'May I live to see it,' said her mum.

'You will,' said Danielle. '*And* when she's done it you're going to take me to McDonald's and buy me a Big Mac.'

Danielle's mum doesn't approve of McDonald's, so Danielle never gets to go there. It's a sore point.

'If you say so,' said her mum, not thinking.

After that, Danielle and her friends spent a lot of time dreaming up ways in which Chuck could save the universe so that Danielle could get her Big Mac. This worried Chuck. She didn't know what the universe was, or what saving it meant. She only knows a few words, such as 'Come' and 'Sit' and 'NO!' She might just about learn what a Big Mac was, if Danielle wanted to teach her.

But she's pretty good at feelings. She even kind-of-feels meanings, so in her tiny whippet brain she vaguely understood that she was supposed to do something, only it was much too difficult for her.

That's quite enough to worry Chuck.

One day, after school, Danielle took Chuck round to have tea with Jenny. She lives in a different part of the town, where all the houses have large front gardens.

Jenny's sister Beth told them to go and have tea someplace else. Beth is almost grown up. She thinks.

'Gran's coming to meet Jake,' she said. 'I don't want you two around, let alone that wimpet.'

'Chuck's a *whippet*,' said Danielle.

'She's a wimpet if ever I saw one,' said Beth. 'Now scram!'

'Can't I wait and watch Gran swooning when she sees Jake?' said Jenny.

'Gran doesn't know he's coming,' said Beth. 'She's going to be sitting here having a lovely, calming cup of tea, and Jake's going to show up with a message as if he's not anyone special, and I'm going to offer him a cup, just being polite, and he's going to get talking with Gran while he's drinking it – I've told him to suss out the French Impressionists – and in a minute or two she's going to forget about the pink hair and the leathers and she'll be thinking, what an absolutely delightful young man. So scram.'

'He's going to have to drink that tea real slow,' said Jenny.

'Will. You. Please. Scram!' said Beth.

'If you promise to mend Podge by the weekend,' said Jenny.

'Promise,' said Beth.

'You promised twice already,' said Jenny.

'Promise. Promise. Promise. That makes six,' said Beth.

'OK if we have tea in the pear tree?' said Jenny.

'I suppose so,' said Beth. 'But keep your heads down. You're doing a late class at school, because if she knows you're here she'll want you in to coo over, and Jake won't have a chance.'

So Jenny and Danielle got some tea together and went out into the garden. They found a neat place for Chuck under the living-room window, where she couldn't be seen from anywhere, told her to lie down, and put the loop of her lead over a twig. Chuck lay down and went to sleep, and Danielle and Jenny climbed into the pear tree, where Jenny had a tree-house, and you could look out all up the road without being seen.

'What's the matter with Podge?' said Danielle.

'He had an accident,' said Jenny. 'His stomach keeps coming out.'

'Which way will your gran come?' said Danielle.

'Out of the alley up there. You can just see the bollard,' said Jenny. 'She'll be late, of course.'

They kept a lookout while they had tea, and Jenny's gran didn't come and didn't come, and then at last there she was so they ducked down out of sight and peeked between the leaves until she reached the gate.

Inside the house Beth was having a final look round the living-room to see that everything was neat and tidy. Just as she heard the gate click she noticed Podge on the window-sill behind the curtain with his stomach all coming out.

Oh no, she thought. Gran will be all upset and she'll go on and on about how she gave him to Mum but no-one looks after him now, and she won't be in any kind of mood for pink hair and leathers.

She heard the gate-latch click.

Quick as a flash she dropped Podge out of the window.

Chuck heard the gate-latch. It woke her up. It must mean something was coming to get her. She started trembling. And a motorbike noise up the road! Coming to get her too!

Then Podge came thumping down out of the sky, straight in front of her!

Chuck bolted.

The twig which the lead was fastened to broke.

Round the corner of the house.

Up the garden path.

Gate open.

Person in the gateway, but it didn't matter. Just room between person's legs.

No there wasn't.

But she whizzed through somehow, and nobody fell on her this time . . .

About fifty metres up the pavement it struck Chuck that there was something wrong with her lead. It didn't have an end.

Another fifty metres and it *still* didn't have an end.

This was really frightening.

Leads have ends. You hit them when you bolt. That's the system.

Worse still, just up the road there was a really menacing bollard waiting to get her.

She stopped dead, turned round, and started to bolt back.

But she *still* didn't hit the end of her lead. And something decidedly threatening was happening back at the gateway. A motorbike. A person fooling around on the ground. Another person bending over that person. Another person running up to join in.

There wasn't anywhere else to bolt to and the

lead system had completely broken down, so Chuck gave up and sat down and just trembled. It was the best she could do. At least Podge wasn't coming to get her any more. He must have taken a wrong turning.

Through the leaves Danielle and Jenny saw Jenny's gran go over. Jenny completely forgot what Beth had said about keeping out of sight, and started to climb down to go and help her gran. Danielle was desperate to go and find Chuck before she got lost or was run over, but it was a tricky climb down and she had to wait for Jenny, so she saw everything that happened.

Jenny had hardly started when a motorbike came roaring up and a bloke with a Guns N' Roses crash helmet jumped off and ran over to Jenny's gran and began to pick her up. Another bloke came running up as if he was going to help but instead he bent down and sprinted on, and Jenny's gran started shrieking, 'My bag! He's got my bag!' The Guns N' Roses bloke looked round and yelled and dashed for his bike and went roaring off.

Chuck watched the man running. She almost bolted again, but she was too scared of the bollard, so she just cowered out of his way. He ran on past. That was all right.

But then the bike started. It gave a dreadful whippet-eating roar and came to get her. It was far, far worse than the bollard. She bolted.

From the tree-house Danielle watched the bloke with the bag sprinting up the road and the Guns N' Roses bloke roaring after him on the bike. He wasn't quite going to catch him, because the bloke with the bag could swing in to the alley, and the bollard meant the bike couldn't get through . . .

At that moment Chuck came into view.

Whippets are terrifically fast, and Chuck was really streaking, ears flat back, legs a blur. She was going three times as fast as the bloke with the bag. She was just going to race past him.

Only he turned.

Slap in front of her.

There was a gap between his legs.

No there wasn't.

Danielle saw the bloke with the bag go flat on his face and the Guns N' Roses bloke jump off his bike and grab him and take the bag off him and give him a boot up the backside which sent him out of sight down the alley. He picked his bike up and wheeled it back down the road. Beth was out of the house by now, looking after Gran, so Jenny decided she'd better stay out of sight and climbed back up again.

The Guns N' Roses bloke handed the bag to Jenny's gran and took off his crash helmet. He had the most amazing pink hair. He said hello to Beth as if he knew her just a bit and Beth said hello back to him, and they stood around saying thanks and not at all and are you really all right, Gran, and what about a cup of tea and well just a cup, thanks, still making a great act of knowing each other just a bit and looking after Jenny's gran until they got indoors.

As soon as Jenny was out of the way, Danielle climbed down the tree and went to look for Chuck. She found her sitting on the pavement up beyond the alley, still worrying about her lead. Chuck had worked out that *her* end was all right, but there was something missing from the other end. Danielle picked it up and took her back to the garden, where they found Podge. Jenny hid him behind a lavender bush so he couldn't come and get Chuck, and then she and Danielle crouched under the living-room window listening to the talk. The Guns N' Roses bloke, Jake, talked to Jenny's gran about French Impressionists. He must have drunk his tea like Jenny had said, real slow, but in the end he said he'd got to go.

As soon as he was out of the house Jenny's gran said, 'What an absolutely delightful young man, in spite of the pink hair and the leathers.'

Danielle told her mum about it later.

'. . . and of course they'll marry and have lots of children and be happy ever after, and they'll never know they owe everything to Chuck.'

'Everything?' said Danielle's mum, not thinking.

Danielle saw her chance.

'Everything!' she cried. 'The whole world and the sun and the moon and the stars and the planets!

The universe! Chuck saves the universe! *And* you owe me a Big Mac!'

'Nice try,' said her mum.

Chuck Versus Jumper

Chuck is confused about cats.

She's confused about a lot of things, but especially cats.

One part of her tiny mind tells her she's supposed to chase them, but another part tells her that they're going to chase her.

And get her.

So she's out on a walk and she sees a cat ahead, up the street, and the first mind-part cuts in—

Something to chase! Wow!

Her ears go up, her tail stiffens, her eyes glisten and she makes herself as tall as she can, walking with prancing steps on the tips of her toes, thrilled.

Now the cat notices her. Most times it thinks *Uh-uh, dog,* and slinks off through a hole in a fence or goes and lurks under a car, and when Chuck gets to the place, she sniffs at it and wants to explore until Danielle yells at her to come on.

But sometimes the cat doesn't notice. Or it's a mean, streetwise cat who knows how to see dogs off. Or it's a normal cat who's met Chuck before and knows it can see *her* off, at least. Anyway, it stays put, crouching low and watching.

Then, as Chuck comes nearer, the second mind-part begins to take over—

Watch it! Some
cats
are
MONSTERCATS!!!

Chuck's ears go back and her tail droops and she sidles along close against the fence, glancing at the cat and away again . . .

Then it puts up its back and snarls, and instantly Chuck's hitting the end of her lead, though Danielle has seen what's coming and has got it short so that no-one falls over.

Then, when they're safely past, Chuck goes on ahead again, almost as if nothing had happened, though actually she's checking all the gateways for Monstercats.

So everyone knew there were going to be problems when Danielle's mum borrowed Jumper to get rid of the mouse. She chose a weekend, so that Danielle could protect Chuck, but even so Chuck spent most of the time hiding under the bath, just to be on the safe side.

The mouse left, so that was OK.

Jumper didn't, and that wasn't.

Jumper had found out he didn't need to worry about Chuck.

He'd also found out how to use the dog-flap.

Chris-across-the-street put it in, so that Chuck could get into the garden for a pee while Danielle was at school and her mum was at work. That's about six hours, and Chuck can last out if she absolutely grits her teeth, but it meant Danielle's mum always had to hurry home to let her out, so it was obviously better for both of them to give her a dog-flap.

Chuck hated it at first. It was a Chuck-trap, of course. With teeth. (It had nipped her tail first time she'd used it, because she was a bit slow.) Even when she'd got the hang of it she used to wait as long as she dared, hoping someone would come home and open the door. Then, at the last possible moment, she'd screw up her nerve and bolt into the garden . . .

Aaaaaaaaaaah!

Danielle and her mum didn't know about this, of course, because they weren't there.

Jumper didn't usually come into the garden in those days. He'd plenty of other gardens to go to when Mrs Birrell put him out for the day, and he'd taken a sniff at this one and thought *Uh-uh, dog,* and so given it a miss.

But after he'd come to deal with the mouse and found out what a wimp Chuck was, he changed his mind. As soon as Mrs Birrell put him out he'd head straight for Danielle's flat, in through the dog-flap, and tell Chuck to scram.

Chuck scrammed.

So Danielle's mum would get home and find Jumper curled up on the sofa and Chuck cowering in the garden. Given the chance they'd have stayed that way till Mrs Birrell rang her special bell to tell Jumper his dinner was ready. But Danielle's mum got home and yelled at Jumper and chased him out, and yelled at Chuck and made her come in. She didn't yell at Danielle, but she got snappy after the first few times and didn't make jokes about giving Chuck away, so Danielle saw it was serious.

They tried a dog-tray but it made Chuck totally miserable. She just *knew* she wasn't allowed to pee indoors.

'I'll see if Cyril has any ideas,' said Danielle's mum.

Cyril works at the lab. His job is to keep the equipment going. He's a complete gadget nerd, and he'll fix anything provided you keep telling him how brilliant he is. Danielle's mum must have really laid it on, because he rigged up what he called a radio lock. There was a little transmitter to go on Chuck's collar and a motor that fitted to the flap.

'Like the doors at Tesco's?' said Danielle, when he came to fix it.

'Nope,' said Cyril. 'They'll open for anyone. This little gizmo is just for the pooch.'

It cost a bit, but Danielle used her savings, and it really worked.

Chuck loved it. She got the hang of it straight off. The flap stopped being a Chuck-trap and became a friendly little door, opening as soon as she came near and waiting for her to get her tail clear before it closed. Wonderful. Clever, clever Danielle, telling the interesting-trouser-man (that's Cyril – he's not a tidy eater) just what to do.

And how to keep the Monstercat out.

'I wish I could have seen him, first few times,' Danielle said. 'Trying to barge through and getting a sore nose.'

But then it all went wrong.

Worse than before.

Danielle's mum was at work and Danielle was at school, and Chuck needed to go into the garden, so she walked to the flap and waited for it to open.

It opened OK.

And the Monstercat came bounding through and curled up on the sofa.

Chuck shot into the garden. When she tried to

come back in, the Monstercat opened one eye and bared one fang and told her to scram.

She scrammed.

Danielle's mum came home and found Chuck cowering in the garden and Jumper asleep on the sofa.

What's more, Jumper hadn't been able to get out, so he'd peed on the curtain.

(Jumper is not a nice cat. Even Mrs Birrell says he isn't a nice cat. 'Why don't you get rid of him?' people ask. 'You can't get rid of someone just because they aren't nice,' she says.)

The whole room stank. They drenched that bit of curtain with bicarb, which made it better, but you could still smell it a bit. Danielle's mum really minded.

'It was just bad luck,' said Danielle, when they'd worked out how it must have happened. 'He'd have to be waiting there at exactly the right moment. It's a thousand to one. It *can't* happen again.'

'Better hadn't,' said her mum.

But it did.

And again.

Not every day, anything like. Maybe a whole week went by, no trouble. But then two days running Danielle's mum would get home, and Jumper would be curled up on the sofa, and there'd be pee on the curtain. Horrible.

'It's all right, darling,' she said. 'I'm not going to ask you to give Chuck away. I promise. It's my fault, anyway, for letting the brute in here in the first place. I'd sooner have the mouse. *But something has got to be done!*'

Danielle asked Chris-across-the-street.

'Beyond me,' he said. 'I could try running him over with the van. Keep my eyes skinned, shall I?'

Cyril wasn't interested. In fact he was quite snappy with Danielle's mum, as if it was her fault his gizmo wasn't working any more.

And no-one else could think of anything.

This went on, oh, about a couple of months, and then one evening after tea there was a ring at the door. Danielle went and opened it. Mrs Birrell was standing there.

'May I come in?' she said. 'I've had an idea about your little dog and Jumper.'

Danielle showed her into the living-room and Danielle's mum said hello. Chuck was hiding behind the TV where she goes for visitors until she has made quite sure they aren't the kind who eat whippets. Then she crept out, tremble, tremble, tremble, and said hello too.

They didn't know Mrs Birrell very well. She was just someone they met in the street. She is a sharp-looking oldish woman who used to be a chemistry teacher at a university. She has the most amazing front garden, all hung up in pots so that Jumper can't lie on it. It's about the size of a single bed and it's nothing to look at, fuzzy plants with dull little flowers, but when you walk past it on a sunny day it smells like Paradise. It's for anybody blind who happens by, Mrs Birrell says.

Now she asked if Jumper was still being a nuisance and she looked at the flap and the curtain and said had they tried bicarb. Then she took a small bell out of her bag.

'Jumper's a really greedy cat,' she said. 'You've heard me ringing my bell for his dinner? He always comes. So if I want to take him to the vet, or something like that, I ring my bell and he's there in a flash. Of course he hates the vet, but he can't bear the idea that he might be missing his dinner.'

'I see him streaking along the top of the wall,' said Danielle.

'That's right,' said Mrs Birrell. 'I've had a bit of trouble finding a bell which sounds exactly the same, but I think this one will do. My idea is that you have it fixed so that it rings whenever the flap opens, and that will fool Jumper into thinking it's dinner-time. I'm not sure that it will work, but it's worth a try.'

Danielle thanked her very much and went to see Chris-across-the-street about fixing the bell.

He laughed and said, 'No problem.'

Mrs Birrell kept Jumper shut in all Saturday morning so that Chuck could get used to the bell. The first time it rang she shot off behind the TV, but Danielle coaxed her and coaxed her until she decided that the ring wasn't a sinister warning about the flap having teeth after all, or something. She got it in the end.

They had things to do on Saturday afternoon, but on Sunday morning Danielle waited by the window until she saw Jumper leap down into the garden.

Then she firmly shoved Chuck out through the flap.

The bell rang.

Jumper shot across the garden, up the wall and away, looking for his dinner.

'Magic!' cried Danielle.

'It won't last,' said her mum. 'The brute will get used to it.'

But it did last. Or rather . . .

Now, this is the truly surprising bit.

The bell worked for a while in the way it was meant to. In fact, Danielle once saw it working twice in one go. She was home because she'd had flu and she was playing a video game her friend Billy had lent her, so she hadn't noticed how time had gone by when Chuck needed to go out, and used the flap. Danielle heard the bell ring and looked up and saw Jumper streaking along the top of the wall in case it was dinner-time.

Then Chuck must have found something interesting to sniff in the garden, so by the time she came back in Jumper was mooching back along the wall in a frustrated kind of way, but as soon as the bell rang he turned right round and streaked off, in case it really meant dinner *this* time.

But mostly, of course, Chuck used the flap when Danielle and her mum weren't there, so they didn't notice anything special except that Jumper hadn't been in again to pee on the curtains, so it wasn't till the holidays that Danielle saw this amazing thing.

Her mum was at work. Danielle was watching TV with Chuck on her lap, braving her up for the vacuum cleaner.

(Chuck hates the vacuum cleaner. It gets out of its lair in the hallway and goes roaring round the flat looking for whippets to chew up, while heroic, valiant Danielle holds on to its tail and tries to stop it. Chuck hides under the bath until Danielle has wrestled the brute back into its lair. Danielle says it's not good for Chuck to get that scared, so she braves her up by letting her sit on her lap before she vacuums. Her mum says it's just an excuse for watching TV instead of getting on with the vacuuming.)

Chuck seemed to be asleep, but suddenly she looked up, stared at the garden door, slipped off Danielle's lap and stalked across to the flap.

Danielle stood up to see what was going on, and saw Jumper just settling down in a patch of sun at the back of the garden.

Chuck paused in front of the flap. She knew the right distance to an inch by now. She took one step nearer, to make it open, and charged through.

She streaked across the garden, straight at Jumper.

Jumper shot up the wall, and away.

Chuck barked.

Not a silly little puppy-yip, but a BIG DOG YAP!

(Danielle didn't know she could do that.)

And only then did Danielle realize that when the flap had opened *the bell hadn't rung*!

She went out and looked at it. The little swinging bit which hit the sides had fallen off and vanished.

So the bell *couldn't* ring.

Perhaps it hadn't rung for weeks.

So Jumper hadn't shot up the wall because he'd thought it might be dinner-time. He'd gone because Chuck had chased him out of her garden. Seen him right off.

What's more, she'd known she could do it. No problem.

Amazing.

'Mrs Birrell's a witch,' Danielle told Jenny that afternoon. 'All that stuff about Jumper wanting his dinner is phooey – that's just so we don't suss out it's a magic bell. Jumper's her familiar, and she's got a magic bell to call him and she gave us a magic bell to send him away.'

'But what if it doesn't ring?' said Jenny.

'It doesn't have to,' said Danielle. 'All you've got to do is shake it.'

'Garden like that, she really might be a witch,' said Jenny.

Chuck doesn't know about magic, of course, but

if she did perhaps she'd agree. She'd say it was a magic bell all right, only its magic was to make Monstercats scoot.

And anything that scoots gets chased. That's the system.

Usually, of course, it was Chuck who did the scooting and getting chased, by motorbikes or paper bags or pigeons or whatever, but there was no reason it shouldn't happen the other way round sometimes.

It had taken several weeks for Chuck to work this out, but when, day after day after day, she'd sneaked out into the garden for a pee, and every single time the Monstercat had scooted, even a thimble-brain begins to think there might be a connection.

So she'd stopped sneaking, and just gone.

And the Monstercat had scooted even faster.

So she'd tried actually rushing out.

Wow!

Making Monstercats scoot was great!

Clever, clever Danielle, getting her that magic bell.

'It doesn't work with other cats, then?' said Jenny. 'I mean that fluffy little one just now, she was slinking along behind you.'

'Of course not,' said Danielle. 'It's just for Jumper. And anyway, she's got to shake the bell to make it work.'

'So what would happen if we met Jumper out here in the street?' said Jenny.

'I don't know,' said Danielle.

Chuck doesn't know either.

She's confused about cats.

CHUCK AND THE THUNDERING HERD

Danielle doesn't know anything about her dad. She knows she has one, but that's all. When she asks about him her mum just shakes her head and sighs and says, 'I'll tell you some time.' But she never does.

'I don't think I mind not having one,' she told Jenny. 'But I really mind not knowing. It's as if there was a bit of me missing. A sort of hole.'

'Why won't she tell you?' said Jenny.

'I don't know. I think she really wants to, but she can't bear to talk about it,' said Danielle.

'And I've got too many dads,' said Jenny. 'It isn't fair.'

She has two. There's the one she lives with, because he's married to her mum. He's called Stephen, and she gets along with him fine.

And there's her Other Dad, who's her real father, so she does her best with him when he comes to take her for a visit, though she knows quite well he'd much rather be out fishing, or doing judo. He's a black belt, which means he's really good, Jenny says.

Still, visits aren't much fun for either of them, which is why Jenny asked if she could bring Danielle along next time. And Chuck, of course.

'Provided it isn't going to be sick in my car,' he said.

'Of course she won't,' said Jenny. 'Chuck's very good about cars.'

She was guessing. Danielle's mum can't afford a car, so Chuck had never been in one since she came from the breeder. She'd been a puppy then, so not very good about anything.

They arranged to meet outside Jenny's house on Sunday morning. Just as they were getting to the gate a car drew up.

Chuck thinks most cars are harmless. Only a few

of them make coming-to-get-you noises, a tyre which goes *swish-swish*, or a rattly fender, or a squeak, or something. This seemed to be one of the harmless ones until, just when they were alongside it . . .

BAAARRRP!

Even Danielle jumped.

Chuck hit the end of her lead so hard that she almost pulled Danielle over. And then, just when

Danielle was getting her balance . . .

BAAAARRRRP!!

Usually hitting the end of her lead once is enough for Chuck. It seems to jerk her out of her panic so that she can just sit there, tremble, tremble, tremble, until she decides that the coming-to-get-you thing must have missed, or taken a wrong turning, or something. But at the second hoot she threw a real wobbly, plunging and threshing against the lead like she used to do when she was a puppy, so that Danielle had to haul her in and pick her up and hold her until she could sense the panic ebbing away.

The driver got out and stood by the car, looking at Jenny's house and then at his wristwatch. He was a stocky, red-faced man with sandy hair, going a bit bald. He was wearing a baggy green and purple jersey. He didn't seem to have noticed what was happening to Danielle and Chuck.

After a bit he leaned into the car.

BAAARRRP!

Chuck gave a violent squirm, but even when she's in a panic she knows that as long as brave Danielle is holding her tight, nothing really bad can happen, so after that one squirm she just huddled there, tremble, tremble, tremble.

Jenny came running out of the house.

'Hi, Dad,' she said. 'Hi, Danielle. Hi, Chuck. I was just putting my shoes on. Dad, this is Danielle. And Chuck. This is Dad.'

She spoke in a quick, bright gabble, trying to pretend nothing was wrong.

'Hello, there,' said the man. 'That animal had better not throw up in my car.'

Danielle was tempted to say she wasn't sure, because then perhaps she wouldn't have to go. She didn't like Jenny's Other Dad at all, so far. But she decided it wouldn't be fair on Jenny.

'She hasn't had anything to eat,' she said. 'And I've got lots of newspaper and plastic bags.'

In fact Chuck had the best of the journey, because she settled onto Danielle's lap, where nothing bad could happen to her even in a whippet-eating car, and went to sleep. Danielle sat in the back so that Jenny could talk to her Other Dad.

Danielle spent the journey being scared. Jenny's Other Dad drove very fast. If there was another car in front of him he got right up close to it and flashed his lights and swore at the driver until it got out of his way. Jenny chatted and prattled but Danielle could tell she wasn't having a good time either.

Jenny's Other Dad lived in a one-storey brick house near the edge of another town. There was lawn all round, and a climbing-frame and a swing, and a caravan parked against the hedge. He had a wife, whom Jenny called Mary, and twin boys, Dick and Derek, about four. Mary was almost-fat, with smile-dimples, but she was busy getting dinner ready and stopping the boys fighting, so Danielle and Jenny took Chuck out onto the lawn and fed her, and then gave her a walk round the block.

'Dad's in a mood,' said Jenny. 'He's usually better than this.'

The mood seemed to get worse. He yelled at the twins for behaving the way small boys do behave, wriggling and wanting to play with Chuck and acting up in front of the visitors, and between yelling he griped at Mary as if it was her fault.

After a bit of this she said, 'Why don't you take the girls out to the canal this afternoon? You could do a bit of fishing and they could take the doggie for a walk along the canal.'

'Oh, yes,' said Jenny at once. 'That would be great.'

'All the spaces will be gone,' said Jenny's Other Dad, but he cheered up, gobbled the rest of his food and rushed off to get his fishing gear together. Jenny and Danielle offered to help with the washing-up, but Mary said, 'No thanks. You're much more use getting that great lummock out from under my feet.'

The canal was a few miles away along twisty lanes. Jenny's Other Dad went whizzing round the corners as if there couldn't possibly be anything coming the other way. There was, twice, and he had to jam on his brakes and screech to a stop. Then he made rude gestures at the other drivers as he went by.

They came to a humpy bridge with cars parked along by it, and got out. Jenny's Other Dad got his fishing gear out and led the way down beside the bridge on to the towpath. The canal was very still, and stretched away between tall hedges. The path was firm and dry and wide enough for two people, with a steep, narrow bank between it and the water. Every few yards along the bank there was a man sitting on a stool, with a couple of rods poking out over the water beside him. The rods were on special stands, so that he didn't need to hold them. Some of the men had huge umbrellas up over them, to keep the sun off. Or the rain, perhaps. Hard to tell, as it wasn't a particularly sunny or rainy day.

Anyway, Chuck didn't like the umbrellas at all. The first one they came to, she hit the end of her lead with a bang, so Danielle picked her up and carried her past the rest.

'Too many blanking idiots down this end,' said Jenny's Other Dad. 'We'll take a look round the bend.'

The canal curved, and just beyond the bend there was a fence across the path with a stile, with a footpath-sign pointing ahead. But there was also a notice saying 'NO FISHING BEYOND THIS POINT'.

'Blank that for a lark,' said Jenny's Other Dad.

He climbed the stile and got out his stool and started to get his gear out. Danielle put Chuck down and let her jump the stile a few times, for fun.

'OK, kids,' said Jenny's Other Dad. 'Got a watch, Jenny? Be back in a couple of hours. Don't get lost. You'll be OK if you stick to the canal.'

So Jenny and Danielle and Chuck set off. When they looked back before the next bend, Jenny's Other Dad had his rods set up and his Walkman over his ears and was just settling down to fish. They walked on round the curve.

'I wish Stephen was my real dad,' said Jenny.

She seemed a bit depressed, so of course Danielle

was too. The canal made it worse. It seemed so empty, as if there was nobody around for miles except Jenny and her and Chuck. It made her feel nervous.

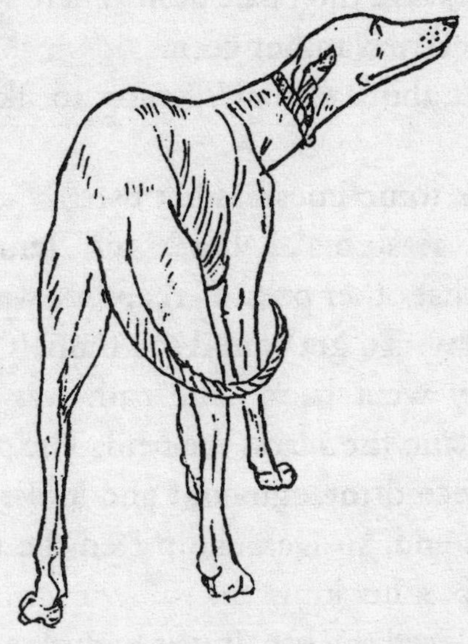

Chuck didn't feel nervous. She thought the canal was lovely, and full of thrilling new smells. She strutted ahead with her ears pricked, looking as if she was certain something to chase was going to pop out of the hedge right in front of her.

They came to a gate, with a footpath-sign pointing off across the fields. The towpath went on ahead, though, so they did what they'd been told and stuck to it, but then, only a couple of bends further on they came to a place where the canal and the towpath went into a tunnel.

They stopped at the entrance and looked. The other end was a tiny, pale blob. There seemed to be a lot of darkness in between.

'I don't think Chuck's going to like this,' said Danielle.

(Chuck sometimes has her uses.)

'Don't let's make her,' said Jenny quickly. 'There's that other path. Perhaps we were meant to go that way. To get round the tunnel, I mean.'

So they went back. The path was quite clear, running slantwise across the field. The gate was tied with a piece of orange cord and looked wonky at the other end, so Danielle patted the top bar and said, 'Hup, Chuck.'

Chuck eyed the bar. It was higher than anything she'd ever jumped.

'Come on, Chuck,' said Danielle. 'You can do it. Hup.'

OK, thought Chuck. If Danielle says so.

She gathered herself on to her haunches and sprang, got her front feet on to the bar, scrabbled over and leaped lightly down. The girls climbed after her, and started off across the field.

'Ugh, cowpats,' said Jenny.

'Oh, oh, cows,' said Danielle.

The cows were black and white, over on the other side of the field, a bit away from the path. Some of them were standing up and eating, but most of them were lying down.

'They don't look very big,' said Jenny. 'I think they're just calves.'

'We'll be all right if we've got Chuck with us,' said Danielle. 'Cows don't like dogs. I saw a little dog chasing cows all over the place on *Emmerdale*.'

(They were both right, and both wrong. These cows were half-grown heifers. Jenny and Danielle were town kids, so they didn't know how inquisitive heifers can be. And cows really don't like dogs. It's an instinct from long, long ago, when cows were still wild, and the only dogs around were wolves. If you're a wild cow, and a wolf happens along, the best thing you can do is get together with the rest of your herd and charge it down. Jenny and Danielle didn't know that.)

They started off along the path. When they were about a third of the way across the field one of the cows looked round and stared at them.

'Watch it, cow,' said Danielle. 'When Chuck saves the universe and I get my Big Mac, you might be it.'

'She'll be a very old cow by then,' said Jenny.

Now several of the cows were staring at them. The lying-down ones were heaving to their feet. All staring . . .

Beginning to move . . .

Fanning out . . .

'We'd better go back,' said Jenny.

'Walk, don't run,' said Danielle.

They turned and walked, fast as they could, but looking back over their shoulders they saw that it wasn't fast enough. The cows were trotting, heads down, shoulder to shoulder, like a moving wall.

The girls' nerve broke, and they ran.

It still wasn't fast enough. Danielle could hear the drumming hooves. She tripped, fell, let go of the lead . . .

Just in time. As she scrambled to her feet the cows came thundering past. None of them touched her. Or Jenny, who was still running along the path. It was Chuck they were after, and Chuck had raced away as soon as her lead was free, swerving off to one side. She was far faster than the cows, of course, streaking away . . .

Danielle and Jenny raced for the gate, climbed it, and turned, gasping.

'Chuck!' yelled Danielle. 'Chuck!'

For a moment she couldn't see her, but she knew where she must be by the way the cows were charging. Yes, there she was, a small, fawn blob, racing across the middle the the field . . .

'Chuck!'

Perhaps she heard, or perhaps she just swerved that way. Danielle climbed on to the middle bar of the gate, balanced herself and waved and called, and now Chuck had seen her and came racing towards her.

But the cows came too, cutting the corner . . .

'Hup!' cried Danielle. 'Hup!'

But Chuck couldn't. She'd forgotten how. All she knew was running. She scuttled along the fence, panting, tongue lolling out, looking for a hole.

The cows were coming.

'Run, Chuck! Run!'

She'd heard them too, and was racing away along the hedge.

Off they charged, after her.

'Get the gate open!' shouted Danielle. 'We'll let her through and shut it before they come.'

They scrabbled with the orange cord, undid it at last, and heaved the gate open. It swivelled half sideways on its wonky hinges, but Danielle hardly noticed. She ran out into the field and looked for Chuck.

The cows were charging in towards the corner. And there was Chuck, trapped, right in the corner, scuttling to and fro, looking for a hole.

'Chuck!' screamed Danielle. 'Chuck!'

And this time she did hear her. Definitely, Danielle said afterwards.

The cows were almost on her, but she looked towards Danielle's voice and ran straight at them, jinked through a gap and came streaking across the grass.

The cows turned to follow.

Danielle raced for the gate, but Chuck was there first. With a gasp of relief Danielle saw her whip through the gap.

She ran to help Jenny with the gate.

It wouldn't shut.

It was too heavy for them, and it had jammed itself on its hinges somehow.

They were still wrestling with it when the herd came streaming through.

Aghast, panting, they stood and watched the cows thundering down the towpath after Chuck. They disappeared round the bend.

'Oh, oh,' said Jenny, and pointed.

There was a man running across the field, shouting. There was no point in running away, so they waited.

He was a big man, red-faced, panting, furious.

'What the hell do you think you're doing, letting a dog loose in a field of heifers?' he yelled.

'She wasn't loose,' said Danielle. 'The cows charged us and I fell over.'

'And we were on the path,' said Jenny.

'Out of the way,' snapped the man.

They stood clear and he lifted the gate bodily and heaved it right open, and then propped it so that it blocked the towpath, and when he fetched the cows back they'd have nowhere to go except into the field.

Without even looking at the girls he marched off down the canal.

They followed. Soon they began to hear noises of snorting and trampling and splashing, and when they came round the bend they saw a lot of cows milling around by the fence with the stile.

Two of the cows were in the canal.

So was Jenny's Other Dad.

There was no sign of Chuck.

Jenny's Other Dad had been peacefully fishing, and he hadn't heard any of the rumpus because of his Walkman. He hadn't even noticed when Chuck had come racing past and jumped over the stile.

The first he knew was when a mass attack of cows came hurtling down on him and barged him into the river. Two of the cows had fallen in with him and the rest were trampling around on his fishing gear.

It was perfectly obvious what he'd been doing.

Now the big man really blew his top. He yelled and swore at the cows and drove them back up the path. The two in the water got frantic about being left behind by their friends and managed to scrabble up the bank. Jenny and Danielle gave Jenny's Other Dad a heave out, and then Danielle climbed the stile and went to look for Chuck.

She found her a little way down the path, panting with exhaustion and staring at a really menacing umbrella. She certainly wasn't going past that without Danielle to look after her. She wasn't worried about the cows any more. They must have taken a wrong turning.

Danielle picked her up and hugged her with relief. She could feel the little heart hammering away, but Chuck licked Danielle's face in a glad-to-see-you-where-have-you-been way and lay there, panting.

Danielle waited. She expected the other two to collect the fishing gear and leave before the man with the cows got back, but they didn't, so she went cautiously round the bend to see what was keeping them.

She found Jenny sitting on the stile, Jenny's Other Dad standing in the path with his arms folded and his fishing gear beside him, and the man with the cows striding back towards him.

As soon as he was in earshot, the man with the cows started to bawl Jenny's Other Dad out for fishing the wrong side of the fence. Jenny's Other Dad bawled right back at the man for keeping heifers in a field with a public footpath where kids might want to go with their dog.

They were both furious. They both knew a lot of language. The man with the cows was much bigger, but Jenny's Other Dad was the better bawler-out.

He was the tops.

He said things which would have got up anyone's nose.

They got up the big man's nose all right.

He lost his cool completely and took a swing at Jenny's Other Dad.

Jenny's Other Dad somehow swayed out of the way, grabbed the man's wrist as it swung past, spun himself round and bent and flipped, and the big man was flying through the air with his arms flailing.

He landed in the canal with a really major splash.

'That's it, then, kids,' said Jenny's Other Dad.

He picked up his fishing gear, climbed the stile

and led the way back down the path.

He was soaked. His fishing had been spoilt. His gear was all trampled, but he drove quietly home, humming to himself. Then he had a shower and changed and came back beaming and said he was going to take them all out to a McDonald's for a Big Mac.

'You don't have to tell your mum,' whispered Jenny while they were getting into the car.

Danielle wasn't even tempted. It wasn't just cheating on her mum. But suppose Chuck did save the universe – somehow, one day – then it would spoil everything if she'd already had her Big Mac in a sneaky kind of way.

'I'll tell him I'm a vegetarian,' she whispered.

'You had fish for lunch,' whispered Jenny.

'Fish doesn't count,' whispered Danielle. 'Karen's a vegetarian, and she has fish.'

'I hope he doesn't mind,' whispered Jenny.

But Jenny's Other Dad only laughed when she asked for a salad, and ordered Big Macs for everyone else. He told Mary everything that had happened as if it was all a wonderful joke, and being barged into the canal by the cows was part of the joke too.

'Was that judo you did to him?' asked Danielle.

'Judo it was, kid,' said Jenny's Other Dad. 'You ought to try it.'

'Mum keeps talking about it,' said Danielle. 'She says women ought to be able to look after themselves, but she hasn't got around to doing anything yet.'

'You ask my friend Perry,' said Jenny's Other Dad. 'Don't wait for your ma. Do it yourself and tell her she can come along if she wants. Perry's an A-one teacher, and he can't be more than a bus ride from where you are. I'll give him a call when we get home, tell him you'll be ringing. You too, Jenny, and I'll pay for the pair of you. Right?'

When they got back, he went into the house to fetch them Perry's number before driving Jenny and Danielle home. While he was doing this Mary said in a quiet voice, 'I want to tell you something, Jenny. Your dad's a really nice, sweet guy. Only he gets a lot of hassle in his job, and he can't blow his top because part of the job is to stand the aggro. You couldn't have done him a better turn than letting those cows push him into the canal, so he could take it out on the farmer.

'And another thing. If ever you're in trouble – doesn't matter if it's all your fault, doesn't matter if you've been really silly or bad – he'll be on your side, no question. Just try and remember that next time you find him in an iffy mood, like he was this morning.'

'Thank you, Mary,' said Jenny. 'I'll remember.'

Chuck Holds the Fort

Danielle's mum said she was going to give Chuck away.

Yes, again.

It happens most weeks, actually.

This time it had been because of the man with the paper bag and the boy on the skateboard. OK, the man shouldn't have scrunched the paper bag just as Chuck was passing, and the boy shouldn't have been skateboarding backwards, aiming for the gap between the woman with the little dog and the shop front, but . . .

'Was he all right?' said Danielle.

'Yes, but the peaches weren't,' said her mum. 'He landed in them.'

'You can't give her away,' said Danielle. 'She's much too useful.'

'Useful?' said Danielle's mum. 'Do you know what the word means?'

'She'll keep the burglars out while we're at judo,' said Danielle. 'I saw it on TV. If you've got a dog they give you a miss.'

Danielle's mum choked on her tea. By the time

they'd cleaned her up they'd found something else to argue about.

Chuck didn't understand about judo but she soon found out what it meant because there was a bag in the hallway, and a bag in the hallway meant Danielle and her mum going away for ever.

(They'd gone for a whole two days, once, to a family wedding, and Mrs Webb upstairs had come in and given Chuck her dinner and tea. Those two days had been for ever, as far as Chuck was concerned, and *they'd* started off with a bag in the hallway.)

Chuck's answer was to try a crust-magic. Danielle bakes special crusts for her, from stale wholemeal bread, and gives them to her after meals to clean her teeth. She adores them, but she doesn't gobble them up the way she does the actual meals. If things are all right she takes the crust and lies down under Danielle's chair and slowly nibbles her way round the edges until it's all gone and then licks up the crumbs.

But if something's wrong she doesn't eat her crust. She takes it and puts it somewhere. And then Danielle has to fetch it and let Chuck come grovel, grovel, grovel, to her feet, so that Danielle can stroke her neck and tell her that everything's all right and she's a good, brave whippet and it's not her fault, whatever it is. (Usually Danielle has no idea.)

Then Chuck takes her crust and eats it somewhere, but not under Danielle's chair. Oh no. That's only for days when everything's all right.

Danielle says this is crust-magic. Chuck is offering a sacrifice of her favourite thing, if only whatever she's bothering about won't happen.

Danielle's mum says it's just Chuck's sneaky way of getting a little extra fuss and attention.

Anyway, judo evenings, Chuck started taking her crust behind the swing-bin in the kitchen, because she'd seen the bag in the hallway. And then Danielle would get it and there'd be the grovelling and the neck-stroking and she'd take it out and eat it right slap next to the bag. It happened the very first evening they went, so just as they were setting off Danielle picked her up and gave her a hug and said, 'Now, you've got to hold the fort, Chuck. Don't let any burglars in.'

And when they got back she said, 'See, Mum? No burglars.'

It happened week after week like that.

Chuck had no idea what burglars were, of course, but after a while, although it was only

Danielle's joke, she somehow worked out that something horrible might be coming to the flat while Danielle and her mum were gone for ever, and she was supposed to stop it.

So as soon as they were gone she checked round the flat for a good place for not letting burglars in.

Under the bath would have been best, but they usually left the bathroom door shut.

Under the sofa?

That used to be a very good place when she was a puppy, but then somehow the sofa's legs had got shorter and she couldn't get under any more. Still, she checked it every week, in case they'd got longer again, but they hadn't.

So she went and curled up small behind the TV, but it was bare boards there so after a while she lay down in her basket and trembled a bit, and then she was asleep.

And then Danielle and her mum came back, and Danielle told her how clever and brave she was, not letting any burglars in.

So the crust-magic, if that's what it was, worked.

But then there came a dreadful evening when Danielle and her mum put their coats on and Danielle said the usual things about not letting any burglars in, and they left.

For ever, of course.

So Chuck checked the bathroom door and the sofa and the place behind the TV and was just settling down in her basket when it dawned on her that something was terribly terribly wrong.

There hadn't been a bag in the hallway!

She hadn't done her crust-magic!

Danielle and her mum had gone for ever!

Burglars were coming!

She must have trembled for at least two minutes before she fell asleep.

The burglar got in through the bathroom, somehow.

Probably up through the loo. Chuck didn't trust that loo. The bath was friendly, but the loo made coming-to-get-you noises, though Danielle and her mum were always careful to shut the door before it made them, so that it couldn't come rushing round the flat after Chuck, like the vacuum cleaner.

Anyway, she heard a click and a rattle. Footsteps! A person.

The bathroom door! The person was letting the loo out!

No, not yet. Footsteps in the hallway.

Coming to the living-room door!

Chuck bolted.

She bolted like she used to when she was a puppy, under the sofa.

Its legs had got longer.

No they hadn't, only she'd shot in so fast that she'd actually forced herself almost right under before she stuck.

She lay there, tremble, tremble, tremble.

The door opened.

The centre light went on.

Feet. Big, big feet.

A male person – she could tell by the smell.

The feet went out. Other doors opened and closed. There were clinkings and water noises from the kitchen.

Chuck stayed where she was, because she was

stuck. At least there was room to tremble. And now she knew what burglars were. They were male persons with big feet. Of course they ate whippets.

After a long, long while (as long as it takes to boil a kettle) the feet came back, bringing the smell of hot person-drink along with them. The TV went on. The feet crossed to Danielle's mum's chair. The burglar started to sit down.

He stopped.

He came over to the sofa, and bent down. Chuck could smell his breath.

'Hello, there,' he said.

Chuck *almost* peed on the floor in her terror. He'd seen her! Her tail must be sticking out! No, it couldn't be, because here it was right in under her belly, which is the proper place when you're terrified. Ears right back, tail right under, tremble, tremble, tremble – that's the drill. She tried to scrabble herself further in.

'Stuck, then?' said the burglar.

His hand groped, found her leg, her neck.

The sofa rose.

She was hauled out, lifted and carried back to Danielle's mum's chair.

This was it! He'd got his drink, and now he'd got his supper.

Whippet.

He sat down, holding her firmly on to his lap.

'Relax, I'm not going to eat you,' he said.

(Burglars just say that. Then they eat you.)

'You must be Chuck,' he said.

He scratched behind her ears in the right place, still holding her down with his other hand. She didn't exactly relax. The moment she got the chance she'd streak for the bath. Or somewhere. But meanwhile, being scratched behind the ears wasn't *quite* as bad as being eaten.

So she lay there, tremble, tremble, tremble . . .

. . . and dreamed of chasing Jumper all over the park . . .

. . . and the front door clicked!

The burglar had let go of her while she was asleep. She streaked.

Door shut.

Round behind sofa. Try the other lot of legs . . .

'Hello,' said Danielle's mum's voice. 'Did we leave the lights on?'

Chuck forgot about the other lot of legs and crept back to the corner of the sofa and peered round. The burglar was standing up, ready for them. He looked ENORMOUS!

(Chuck was mainly used to Danielle and her mum, who aren't that tall.)

Danielle and her mum were coming towards the door!

They didn't know about the burglar!

She had to warn them!

She did the bravest thing she'd ever done in her life.

She barked.

yip

'What on earth was that?' said Danielle's mum's voice.

'Chuck's caught a burglar,' said Danielle's voice.

As the door opened, the burglar raised his arms above his head.

'Told you so,' said Danielle.

'It's a fair cop,' said the burglar.

'Didn't you get my message about meeting you?' said Danielle's mum. 'How did you get in?'

'Bathroom window,' said the burglar. 'Honestly, sis, it's an absolute invitation to larceny. I'll put a safety catch on it for you tomorrow.'

Then they did the kissing-thing and talked all at the same time and laughed a lot, while Chuck watched from the corner of the sofa feeling more and more confused, until Danielle picked her up and hugged her and said, 'It's all right, Chuck. You're a brave, burglar-catching heroine. And now what we're going to do is keep him here and train him not to be a burglar, just like we trained you not to pee on the floor.'

Chuck had no idea what she was talking about, of course, but actually, as the days went by, it did seem a bit like that. Danielle and her mum gave the burglar his food, like Danielle did for Chuck, only he had it off the table and not the floor, because he was bigger. And Danielle and Chuck took him to the park and showed him how to chase balls, only he liked throwing them instead of chasing them, which was all right by Chuck because he could throw a long, long way.

And he had a pet name, like Chuck, only his was Ron, and Danielle called him 'Uncle Ron', like she sometimes called Chuck 'Stupid Chuck'.

He slept on Danielle's bed, like Chuck usually did, but there wasn't room for Danielle too so Danielle and Chuck slept on the sofa. That was fine by Chuck.

Extra-fine.

Because, in the morning, first Danielle's mum went off to the thing called work, and then Danielle and Chuck got up and Danielle had her breakfast and Chuck had a crust and Danielle went off to the thing called school.

But the burglar didn't do anything at all. He stayed in bed.

What's more, he slept with the door open.

That meant Chuck could slip into the room and jump up on to the bed and lick his ear to remind him she was keeping an eye on him. Then she'd curl up against his back and they'd both sleep till dinner-time, when Danielle's mum came home.

He left after a bit (because he was cured of burgling, Danielle said, but actually it was to join an oil-exploring company in Indonesia) and Danielle went back to sleeping in her own room. But she leaves the door shut when she goes to school, because Chuck's never allowed on beds unless there's someone in them.

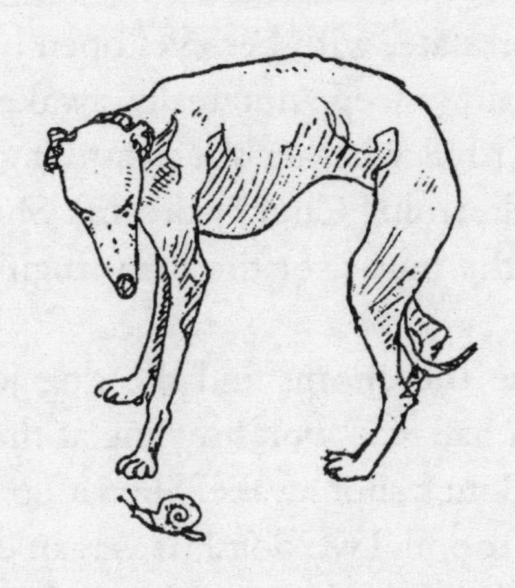

Chuck and the Hard Rock

Chuck has no ear for music.

Any kind of music.

She doesn't seem to notice it's there. Rock, country, grand opera, folk, reggae, cathedral choirs hooting and fluting – they're all just noise, like aeroplanes going over or the ice cream man's bell.

The only time Chuck has paid any attention to music was when Danielle's mum had the radio on, one of those mish-mash programmes, and they played an old record with a singing dog in it. A real dog.

Chuck was lying in her basket. She has this sort

of in-between state, with her eyes open but glazed over, not really asleep, not really awake, so that Danielle can't tell whether she's thinking Chucky thoughts or dreaming Chucky dreams. She paid no attention to the music, or the man singing. Not a twitch.

Then came the chorus and the dog joined in. Weird, like a half-size wolf howling at the moon.

Instantly Chuck shot awake. She sat up, amazed. A dog in the room! Two dogs! (It was an old mono record but this was a stereo system.)

Her head twitched to and fro between the speakers. As the chorus ended she tiptoed over and smelt them in turn.

Not a whiff!

She went back to the middle of the room and stood there, trying to work it out. (By this time Danielle was stuffing a cushion into her mouth so as not to interrupt things by laughing aloud.)

Next time the chorus came round Chuck rushed to and fro between the speakers, or round and round them as if she was chasing an invisible dog round a tree.

Then she went back to her basket and glowered in a deeply suspicious way, and when the third chorus came she lay down with her back to the room, obviously telling these ill-mannered and boringly odourless strangers that she wanted nothing to do with them.

Danielle hasn't decided what kind of music she likes yet. She doesn't get much chance when her mum's around. Her mum says she likes Elton John, but she likes him with the volume turned so far down you wouldn't know it wasn't Axl Rose.

Sometimes, out in the street, they pass an open window with a boom-box turned right up, belting out reggae or heavy metal or hard rock.

'Thank God for Mrs Webb upstairs,' says Danielle's mum.

Mrs Webb upstairs doesn't seem to play anything at all.

Didn't seem to, I mean, because she's moved.

There was an estate agent's board and people coming to view and a 'SOLD' sign, and then – it was half term so Danielle was home – the new people moved in.

Danielle spied on them through her bedroom window. They came in a battered old van. He was an enormous young man, much bigger than Uncle Ron. He had tattoos on his arms and long black greasy hair. He was wearing a sleeveless black shirt with a skull on it.

She was a titchy little woman, in a black leather jacket and jeans, with the most amazing crinkly red-gold hair, masses and masses of it, all the way down to her waist.

The man carried armchairs and things practically under one arm. He looked as if he could have picked up a sofa in his teeth.

There were big cardboard boxes with Hi-fi logos on them. Before they'd finished emptying the van they had the system set up and playing.

Hard rock.

The drum-beat came throbbing down from the ceiling.

Thump thump thump thump thump thump thump.

It didn't bother Danielle. In fact she thought it might have been a bit interesting if she could have heard it not through the ceiling. But she was worried about what her mum would think when she came home.

It didn't bother Chuck at all, of course. It was just noise.

Danielle's mum was hardly into the house before she said, 'What on earth's going on?'

'New people moved in,' said Danielle. 'She's got amazing hair.'

'Well, they're going to have to turn it down,' said her mum.

She went out. Danielle heard the upstairs bell ring. There were voices. They didn't last long.

Her mum came back in. She didn't say anything. She held on to the kitchen table and stood there, looking sick, miserable . . .

'Are you all right?' said Danielle.

Her mum let out a weary breath.

'He swore at me,' she said in a flat voice. 'He told me to buy some ear-plugs.'

After that Danielle minded about the music too,

of course. It wasn't all that loud, really. You didn't have to shout above it. But it went on and on, *thump, thump, thump, thump, thump, thump,* and then a short pause between the tracks, just enough to make you think it might be stopping now, and then, *thump, thump, thump, thump, thump, thump.*

Mum couldn't eat her dinner, though Danielle had done sardines on toast and coleslaw from Tesco's which they both liked. She said she had a splitting headache. She hated rows. It was what the man had said to her, as much as the music. That sort of thing ties people like Danielle's mum in knots inside.

Danielle ate her dinner but she didn't enjoy it. She was too unhappy for her mum.

Chuck didn't eat her dinner, because she knew something was badly wrong and it was all her fault. Everything that goes wrong is her fault. Even when nothing is wrong she knows it's only because wise, brave Danielle is there, putting it right before it can go wrong. And now even Danielle couldn't put the terrible thing Chuck had done right, whatever it was.

She didn't eat her crust either, but took it and hid it behind the TV in case that did any good. It didn't.

As soon as Danielle had finished eating she said,

'Let's take Chuck out to the park.'

'I suppose it will get us out of the house,' said her mum.

Danielle rescued the crust from behind the TV and put it in the ballbag, and off they went. It was a pleasant, bright day, but Danielle's mum couldn't stop brooding about what the man had said, so Danielle couldn't enjoy watching Chuck race after her ball.

Chuck had a good time, because there's only room in her tiny brain for one idea at a time, and ball-chasing fills it right up. Danielle let her get her breath back and then gave her her crust and she gobbled it up, no problem.

But as soon as she had her lead back on, Chuck remembered that something dreadful had happened, and it was all her fault, so she slunk along with her ears flat and her tail down.

Halfway home Danielle's mum stopped in her tracks.

'Right,' she said. 'You take Chuck back and look after yourself, darling. I'm going to the Council. There's a noise abatement officer there. I'll have a word with him. If I'm not going to be home by five I'll give you a ring.'

And off she marched.

When Danielle got home the music was still going on, *thump, thump, thump, thump, thump, thump,* so Danielle put the TV on to shut it out, which it did, almost, but that didn't stop her worrying. In fact it made it worse. Suppose her mum got to see this noise person, and suppose he came along to listen (fat hope!) he'd say it wasn't all that loud, really.

And that was true.

It was only loud if you minded, like her mum did.

She minded worse than ever, after the man had sworn at her.

Every time she heard it she'd remember, and get all screwed up inside.

Perhaps they'd have to move house to get away from it. Danielle loved this flat. She'd lived here ever since she could remember. It was home. Moving would be the end of the world.

So she started feeling sick and screwed up and headachy too.

Chuck lay on her lap, tremble, tremble, tremble, because she could feel how bad things were. And of course it was all her fault.

Then the doorbell rang.

Chuck shot off behind the TV. This was it!

Danielle put the door on the chain before she opened it and peeped through. The woman with the amazing hair was standing on the mat.

'Hello,' she said. 'I'm the new bod upstairs. I thought I'd come and say "Hi".'

Danielle was going to explain that her mum was out, but then she thought perhaps it might be a good idea to start trying to make friends and then say something about the music. If she waited till her mum got back, her mum might go raging in and there'd be a desperate row and it would finish with them turning the music up louder still or something. So she took the chain off and let the woman in, and showed her into the living room.

'My mum's not here,' she said. 'She'll be back later.'

'Well it's nice to meet you,' said the woman. 'I'm Annie.'

'I'm Danielle,' said Danielle. 'And this is Chuck. Come on, Chuck, come and say hello to Annie.'

Very, very bravely Chuck crept out from behind the TV, right down on her belly, grovel, grovel, grovel, tremble, tremble, tremble, ears flat, tail as far as poss between legs, imploring bulgy eyes . . .

'Oh, isn't it cute?' cried Annie. 'Come on, duckie, come and say hello. No need to be scared. I love dogs. What is it? It looks like a toy greyhound.'

'She's a whippet,' said Danielle.

And then . . . it came out before she had time to think . . .

'Actually, it isn't you she's scared of,' she said. 'It's the music.'

Annie laughed.

'It's dire, isn't it?' she said. 'Tell you the truth, I came down here to say sorry about it and it will soon be over. It gives me a headache.'

'Oh,' said Danielle.

'It's Brian,' said Annie. 'I made him turn it down as far as he'd let me. Is it really all that loud? You can hardly hear it with the TV on.'

'Chuck can,' said Danielle. 'And anyway . . .'

She turned the TV off.

Thump, thump, thump, thump, thump, thump.

'I know!' said Annie. 'It's because the speakers are right down on the floor. It acts like a sounding-board. Hold everything. I'll tell him there's a sweet little dog down here who's scared out of her wits. He can put the speakers up on the table or something, for the moment, with rugs under them. I'll be back.'

She shot out. In a couple of minutes Danielle heard the music change. At one moment it was still *thump, thump, thump,* and the next it was *fffp, fffp, fffp.*

Annie came back, looking anxious.

'That's much better,' said Danielle. 'Thank you.'

'Yes, but listen,' said Annie. 'He says someone came to the door and he told her to mind her own business.'

'I'm afraid it was a bit more than minding her own business,' said Danielle.

'Was it your mother?' said Annie.

'Yes.'

'He's a complete, utter . . .' Annie began, but she managed to stop herself saying what she'd been going to. She looked totally furious. Her hair seemed to glint with rage, as if it was full of electricity.

'Will you tell your mother I'm extremely sorry,' she said. 'I'll go and talk to him now.'

She left again. The music stopped completely. There were angry voices, and then footsteps. From her bedroom window Danielle watched the man carry a few more things into the house, and then drive away.

When Danielle's mum came home she looked grim. She'd had no luck at the Council.

'It doesn't matter, Mum,' said Danielle. 'Listen.'

No music through the ceiling. But her mum shook her head.

'It won't last,' she said. 'They've just gone out for a pizza or something.'

'Bet you,' said Danielle.

'What's up?' said her mum, suspiciously.

'Chuck fixed it,' said Danielle, and wouldn't say anything else.

Later the doorbell rang. It was Annie with a pot of chrysanthemums and a box of special health-food chocolates which didn't taste of chocolate because they hadn't got any chocolate in them, to say sorry about Brian having been so rude.

She stayed for a cup of tea and they talked about things like where to go to get a kettle fixed and not letting Jumper into her flat because he'd pee on the curtains.

After a bit Annie explained about Brian.

'We'd been together nearly three years,' she said, 'but then I couldn't take it any more. You know, the rock concerts and the beer and these great hairy macho men. I used to think it was a kick, patching him up after he'd got into a fight, all that, but I've moved on. So I got myself a decent job and told

Brian I was leaving. He didn't like it at all, but there wasn't anything he could do about it. I told him he could keep the van – it's half mine – if he helped me move, and he said OK, but he really took it out on me, sulking like a baby and playing his sort of music as loud as I'd let him, and blinding off at the neighbours. I'm sorry about that. I really am. I hope the little dog's feeling happier now.'

'Oh, yes,' said Danielle. 'Aren't you, Chuck?'

Chuck was. She could feel that the terrible whatever-it-was-which-had-been-all-her-fault had somehow unhappened, and it was Danielle who'd made it unhappen, and there were only the usual things to worry about now.

So when Danielle got up to fill the teapot she let herself be put in Annie's lap and licked Annie's face because it was there and she might as well.

Annie stayed for over an hour, chatting away about health foods and channelling and crop circles and New Age magazines and hatha yoga and so on. Danielle's mum listened and smiled and looked really interested, and every now and then said something which showed she knew what Annie was talking about.

'You really liked her, didn't you?' said Danielle, when Annie had gone.

'I've been there too, you know,' said her mum.

'No, I didn't,' said Danielle.

Her mum looked at her and hesitated.

'I'll tell you some time,' she said.

So Danielle guessed it was something to do with her dad.

Later that evening, thinking about what had happened, she had an idea. In fact she guessed she'd never get a better chance.

'I'm glad we don't have to move,' she said.

'Glad isn't the word,' said her mum.

'Moving would have been the end of the world,' said Danielle.

'Almost,' said her mum.

'So Chuck stopped the end of the world,' said Danielle. 'She saved the universe. Right?'

Her mum grinned and shook her head.

'I said "Almost",' she said.

Chuck at the Show

There is a show every year.

They hold it in the grounds of a grand house on the edge of the town. It all used to belong to Earl Somebody, but the house is now a conference centre and the grounds belong to the town.

It's a really big show. Thousands of people come, from miles away. There are horse trials with famous riders, and pony trials and sheep trials. There are cattle rings and tractor demos and flower competitions and fruit and veg competitions, and a horse-and-carriage parade. There are hundreds of stalls selling things like leather belts and jackknives

and straw dollies and wildlife paintings and pet food, and so on. There are hot dog stands and ice cream stands and Chinese takeaway stands, all that.

Danielle's mum helps at the hospital charity stand. She puts on demos of what she does at the lab, making slides out of blood samples and staining them and then looking in her microscope for things which shouldn't be there.

It's very interesting, but you can't watch it all day, so Danielle meets up with Jenny and Harriet and they wander around, looking. When Chuck was almost a puppy Danielle carried her most of the time, because the show is full of things which might be coming to get her, and she didn't want her bolting between people's legs. But it was very tiring.

So next year she let her walk on her shortest lead, so that she couldn't bolt too far, and she was pretty good. She only really bolted twice, when a steam threshing machine gave a terrific whippet-eating snort, and when a loose balloon came bouncing straight at her.

But you never know with Chuck.

There was this policewoman riding by on an enormous reddy-brown horse, so Danielle shortened Chuck's lead and made her sit to let them go by.

Chuck sat, tremble, tremble, tremble.

The policewoman stopped her horse and looked down, from right up there.

'Nice to see a whippet,' she said. 'My dad keeps whippets.'

So they chatted about whippets. The policewoman said that her dad was a farmer and if a message came for him while he was out in the fields, her mum would write it down and put it in one of his slippers and give the slipper to an old bitch whippet who would take it off and find him.

Danielle was absolutely boggled at the idea of a

whippet doing anything as useful as that. Anything useful at all.

The policewoman had slackened the reins while she was talking and now the horse bowed its head down, looking for grass. It noticed Chuck sitting there, quiet and still, because she's a very obedient dog provided nothing is coming to get her.

The horse peered at Chuck in a good-gracious-what-have-we-here kind of way, and nosed right forward towards her. Danielle thought she was sure to bolt now, because the horse was absolutely huge, but no, she stayed where she was.

Her tail was right between her legs, but it was whipping to and fro beneath her belly, the way it does when she's interested in something but isn't sure if it's allowed.

As soon as the horse's head was close enough, she stretched out her tongue and licked its nose.

The horse snatched its head away, startled, and tried again.

Again Chuck gave its nose a really good lick. (Perhaps it tasted salty.)

The horse snatched its head away again, but Chuck sat where she was, tremble, tremble, tremble, with her tail-tip going to and fro like a buzzer.

The policewoman laughed.

'Plucky little thing,' she said, and rode on.

When Jenny and Harriet came back from buying Cokes, which was what they'd been doing, Danielle told them about it, and they teased Chuck a bit about being a plucky little thing, and then walked on, sucking at their Cokes and looking at this and that. It was getting fairly late when they came to a ring with a sign saying DOG AGILITY TRIALS, so they stopped to have a look.

It was a kind of obstacle course, with jumps and a line of posts to run in and out of, and a seesaw to run up and down, and a ramp, and a tunnel to scuttle through, and a tyre to leap through, and a twisting walkway to balance along, and so on.

The owners weren't allowed to touch their dogs. They had to persuade them to go through or over the obstacles in the right order.

Some of the dogs didn't get it at all, and the owners went frantic trying to get their dog to jump through the tyre instead of running underneath it, or whatever.

But some of the dogs were pretty clever. They obviously thought it was fun. There was a big clock with a hand counting the seconds to show how they were doing, and a scoreboard saying how many points they'd lost for missing obstacles.

'Are you going to let Chuck have a go?' said Harriet.

'She'd think the seesaw was coming to get her,' said Jenny.

'Oh, come on, Danielle,' said Harriet. 'She can do it.'

Danielle was tempted, but she shook her head.

'Course she could do it,' she said. 'But I'm not having her look stupid in front of all these people.'

'What about next year?' said Harriet. 'Yes, why don't you give her a bit of practice and let her try next year? Build her confidence up, right?'

Danielle shook her head again, but she watched a bit longer and then edged round to the entrance, where the organizers seemed to be.

A woman in a wheelchair noticed her. She wasn't specially old but she had absolutely dead white hair which didn't look as if she'd brushed it for a month.

'Hello, love,' she said. 'I'm afraid you're too late. We aren't taking any more entries.'

'I didn't want to enter,' said Danielle. 'I don't think Chuck would understand. But will you be having it again next year?'

'I should think so, if I've got anything to do with it.'

'Will it be the same jumps and things?' said Danielle.

'No point in wasting them now, is there?' said the woman.

After that they watched a bit more and Danielle drew a sketch map of the course, and then they went home.

'I've got to make some obstacles,' said Danielle.

'As if we haven't got plenty already,' said her mum.

'It's for Chuck to practise on,' said Danielle, and she explained about the Agility Test.

'Do you want me to help?' said her mum.

This was a tricky one. Danielle's mum likes to help, but she isn't very good at fixing things. She doesn't seem to understand what is strong enough for what, and then she gets stroppy with her fixings because they don't stay fixed. You can't tell her, either.

'It's for something to do in the hols when you're at work,' said Danielle. 'Then we can do things together in the afternoon.'

(Officially Danielle goes to Lily Flyte at Number 4 in the mornings during the holidays, because she's not supposed to be left alone, but mostly she just tells Lily what she's up to, in case the social worker comes round.)

So she started thinking how to make the different obstacles. The jumps were no problem. Chuck is a terrific jumper. Her legs look like matchsticks, but they've got wonderful springing muscles at the top, for running so fast, and they also let her jump like a kangaroo.

And she really enjoys it. All Danielle has to do is pat the top of the park bench or whatever, and say 'Hup' and Chuck goes sailing over. The old cemetery's a good place too, with its different sizes of tombs, so when no-one's around Danielle takes her down there to jump stone bibles and broken pillars and a mourning angel whose wings are just the right height.

But it wasn't all as easy as that.

The line of posts, for instance.

Danielle collected some old Coke cans and took them up to the park and laid them out and led Chuck through several times on her lead, and then 'heeled' her through without the lead and so on.

Chuck got it in the end, and when she understood what Danielle wanted she whizzed through, faster and faster. She really enjoyed it.

But then Danielle and Chuck went with Jenny and her mum to visit Jenny's cousins at the seaside, and Danielle wanted to show off Chuck's new trick, so they laid out a row of swimming things to be the posts.

Oh, no. Swimming things are *quite* different from cans. You can't expect a dog to weave in and out between *swimming things*.

Danielle collected some cans out of a couple of litter bins and Chuck did fine with those. But Danielle realized that posts are probably quite different from cans too, so she'd have to find some posts.

She got lucky with a skip in the next street, which had two long pieces of wood in it. Chris-across-the-street sawed them up to make six posts, which she could stick in the ground in the park.

She was a bit anxious about this as the park

keeper is rather a meanie. It's as if he enjoys thinking of reasons to stop children doing things, such as sticking posts in his grass, but he's not too bad with Danielle because he's got a dog of his own, a collie, and he likes boasting about how clever she is, and how he can make her do whatever he wants just by blowing a whistle, because she's a proper sheepdog. Danielle keeps on the right side of him by saying she's sure Chuck couldn't do *that*, whatever it is.

But she doesn't enjoy pretending to be nice to him, so she used the posts when she couldn't see him around, and carried them to and fro instead of hiding them in the bushes, because if he found them he'd throw them away.

Chuck sussed out the posts after a bit, and whizzed between them just as neatly as she did the cans.

Chris-across-the-street lent Danielle a good plank to make the seesaw and the ramp. It was too heavy for her to carry up to the park so she had to build them on the pavement outside the flat. She used the bathroom stool and some bricks which the builders had left at Number 27.

She put the stool on its side and wedged it up on to one leg with the bricks, so that the opposite

leg was in the air on top. Then she laid the plank across it and led Chuck over it, holding her collar, making sure that the plank tilted r e a l l y s l o w l y when they got to the middle. Chuck didn't see the point at all, even after she'd decided that this wasn't a deadly whippet-trap just disguised as a seesaw, but she knew it was something Danielle wanted so she got it in the end.

For the ramp Danielle stood the stool on its feet and tied one end of the plank to the top and chocked the other end firm on the pavement with bricks. Chuck decided it was another kind of see-saw, so she was a bit surprised when it didn't tilt in the middle and crept on up, waiting for it to do so. Then she got to the top and just jumped down, no problem.

The walkway was not too bad either. Danielle made it with the bricks and more short planks from skips, and Chuck had decided by now that what you did with planks was get on them and walk up them or down them or along them and sometimes they tilted and sometimes they didn't but it all finished up with Danielle making a fuss over you and telling you how brilliant you were so it was worth it.

Jenny's dad (her stepdad, Stephen) hung a tyre from the pear tree in their garden. Chuck was a bit anxious that Podge might be lurking somewhere, but once she'd decided he wasn't, she jumped through the tyre as if she was in a circus act.

The tunnel, though, was HORRIBLE.

Danielle made it out of cardboard boxes from the supermarket. She opened them up top and bottom, put them on their sides, end to end, and arranged the flaps to cover the gaps. This made a pretty good tunnel, except that it took for ever to fix up and by then it sometimes started to rain and she had to take it to bits again before the cardboard got wet. Frustrating.

And Chuck *hated* it.

First time she built it Danielle tied Chuck's lead to the gate and let her watch it being built, so that she'd know it was only cardboard boxes, but as soon as she went to fetch her, she bolted. She hit the end of her lead like a bullet. Wham!

It wasn't a tunnel. It wasn't made of cardboard boxes. It was a horrible, monstrous, whippet-chomping creepy-crawly from outer space! Or somewhere.

Chuck wasn't going anywhere near it!

Absolutely not!

It took Danielle most of an afternoon to persuade Chuck even to sit a few feet away from the thing. Very bravely she sat, tremble, tremble, tremble, and watched Danielle wriggle in at one end and out at the other.

That didn't prove anything. The thing didn't want people to chomp. It wanted whippets.

In the end Danielle took the tunnel to bits and put it away and tried again a few days later.

And again.

And again.

After several more tries Chuck had decided that

she could just about bear to crawl into the tunnel provided Danielle was there first, holding the other end of her lead. Danielle was pretty sure this was against the rules, and anyway it would take ages.

'And besides,' she told Jenny, 'that isn't any good. I'm building up her confidence, aren't I? I don't mind if she doesn't win. That isn't the point. The point is she's got to feel she's having a good time because she's being clever. Right?'

By now it was term-time again, and getting on winter, so she decided to give the tunnel a rest for a bit and try again in the spring. Perhaps by then Chuck might have forgotten about whippet-chomping creepy-crawlies from outer space.

No such luck.

As soon as they started again it was as bad as ever.

Go into that thing without Danielle to help her through?

No way!

Danielle had pretty well decided it wasn't worth the fuss when Chris-across-the-street made a suggestion. He was interested because he's got a dog of his own, a fat old retriever – and besides he's a really good guy. Helpful.

'Tell you what,' he said. 'Why don't you let her have a go at it same time as she does all the other stuff? If she's good at the jumps and all, I mean. Then maybe she'll understand what it's about.'

'I don't think there's room on the pavement,' said Danielle.

'No problem,' said Chris. 'We'll put all your clobber into my van and run it up to the park and lay your course out proper.'

'Oh, yes, please,' said Danielle. 'Let's hope the park keeper doesn't come by. He's a meanie.'

'Always was,' said Chris. 'I knew him at school. Any trouble, and I'll tell him where he gets off.'

So they loaded all the stuff into the van that evening and took Chuck up to the park. Chris was terrific at fixing the obstacles firm, and he'd brought a few bits of spare timber to make jumps with. They laid the course out just the same as it was at the show, according to Danielle's sketch map, and started Chuck off.

She got the idea almost at once and really

enjoyed herself. Danielle had to race to the next obstacle to say 'hup' or 'here' or 'run', and Chuck sailed over the jumps and did the ramp and the poles and the walkway and tyre as if she'd been doing them all her life.

Danielle ran to the seesaw.

'Here,' she cried.

Chuck trotted calmly up, waited for the tilt, and ran on down.

Danielle was already at the tunnel mouth.

'Here, Chuck,' she called. 'Good girl. Run.'

And Chuck ran.

Straight into the tunnel and out at the other end.

It wasn't a chomper from outer space at all.

It was just some old cardboard boxes which Danielle had put together so that Chuck could show the smelly-big-dog-man how brilliant she was.

She was just about to do the course for the third time, to make sure, when the park keeper showed up.

Oh, oh, thought Danielle. Now Chris is going to tell him where he gets off and there'll be a row and Chuck will decide it was all her fault.

But no.

'Hello, hello, what have we here,' said the keeper. 'Obstacles, is it?'

'We're practising for the show,' said Danielle. 'They have an obstacle course there, and I want to enter Chuck this year and I don't want her to make a fool of herself in front of everyone.'

'All right, then,' said the park keeper. 'Let's see her go.'

Chuck sensed that Danielle was nervous about the park keeper, and of course it was Chuck's fault somehow, so the safest thing was to be very, very good, and that meant sitting as often as possible and waiting to be told she was allowed to do the next thing. So instead of whizzing from obstacle to obstacle, she whizzed up to it, stopped, sat, tremble, tremble, tremble, and waited for Danielle to say 'OK' before she said 'Hup' or 'Run' or whatever. This slowed her down a lot.

It was typical Chuck, and Danielle laughed about it when she told her mum later, but she was pretty frustrated about it at the time. She really wanted to show the park keeper how brilliant Chuck could be, because he was always going on about his clever collie.

But this time he never even mentioned his collie. What's more, when Chris and Danielle started taking the obstacles to bits he said, 'You'll be wanting to give her another go, won't you? Why don't you leave that stuff in my compound, save you carrying it up every time. I've got a spare tarp you could put over it.'

'Oh, yes, please. That would be terrific,' said Danielle.

That meant they could practise the whole course several more times without bothering Chris, so by the time the show came round again Danielle was fairly sure that Chuck wouldn't make a fool of herself.

They got there in plenty of time, and the white-haired woman in the wheelchair actually remembered her.

'Giving it a go then, this year?' she said.

'Yes, please,' said Danielle. 'Are we the first? I don't think I want to go first.'

(Just in case Chuck made a mess of it. It would be better if someone else had made a mess of it earlier.)

'Quite right,' said the woman. 'It's much more fun near the end. You'll know what you've got to beat. Put you down for 3.45, shall I, so take care you're back by half-past three. And it's a pound for the entrance fee, please.'

Danielle paid her pound, and then she and Jenny wandered off doing the usual things, watching the ponies jumping and the carriage parade, and wandering among the stalls. They stopped at the hospital stand and told Danielle's mum that Chuck would be doing her test at 3.45, so that she could knock off doing demos and come and watch. On their way back to the dog ring they met Jason from school, and his little sister Rosie, and their mum and dad. Rosie had an Obelix balloon almost as big as herself.

Jason, who's like that, took the balloon from Rosie and made it come and get Chuck.

Chuck didn't hit the end of the lead because there was a man in the way, but he didn't fall over, quite, so it could have been worse.

Danielle was furious. She really didn't want Chuck thinking things were coming to get her just before her big moment. So she wasn't at all pleased when Jason's family decided they'd like to come and watch Chuck doing her stuff.

The others found places at the side, but Danielle went round to the entrance to tell the white-haired woman she was back.

'There's three still before you,' said the woman. 'Watch out for a black and white collie. That'll mean you're next.'

Danielle took Chuck a little to one side to watch. There were quite a few spectators, including a gang of yobs opposite the clock who'd had a bit to drink and were yelling out the seconds as the dogs went round.

There was a funny-shaped wire-haired mongrel doing the course now. It was about halfway round, going over a jump.

'Thirty,' yelled the yobs.

It didn't like the walkway.

'Thirty-five . . . forty . . .' yelled the yobs.

The owner called it on through the tyre, but it didn't like the seesaw either, so, though it finished in fifty-eight seconds it was penalized another thirty for missing three obstacles and finished up on one minute twenty-eight.

The scoreboard said there'd only been three so far under sixty. Fifty-four was the best. That was the fastest Chuck had ever done in the park.

They adjusted the jumps and the ramp right down for the next dog, which was a tubby little dachshund. He was pretty clever, but he was slow, and waddled sedately round, not missing anything. He finished in one minute eight.

Next there was a beautiful red setter which hadn't got a clue and ran out of time while the yobs jeered.

Next there was the black and white collie.

The moment Danielle saw the owner, she knew him.

It was the park keeper.

And his dog was clever all right. The keeper didn't have to run from obstacle to obstacle, telling it where to go next. He stood to one side with a whistle in his mouth and peeped, and the dog seemed to know what to do.

It absolutely raced round. Jump. Ramp. Jump. Poles. Jump . . .

'Done it before,' said the man standing next to Danielle.

'Nah,' said his friend. 'It's a sheepdog, see? Look, it's made a mess of that one. Now he'll bring it back. Betcha.'

What he was talking about was that the collie had missed its footing on a bend of the walkway and fallen off.

The park keeper gave a frantic peep on his whistle, but the collie paid no attention. It skimmed through the tyre, up and down the seesaw . . .

'Forty,' yelled the yobs, as it disappeared into the tunnel.

It finished on forty-two, but they penalized it ten for falling off the walkway, and that meant fifty-two, so it was the best so far.

With her heart beginning to thud Danielle took Chuck to the entrance. The park keeper was just coming out. His eye caught Danielle's, and flickered away, and back.

He smiled.

'Hello, there,' he said. 'Given you something to beat, right?'

In the flicker of his glance, in the tone of his voice, Danielle saw and heard that the man beside her had been right.

The collie had done it before.

The park keeper hadn't been able to call it back when it fell off the walkway because the whistle-peeps had been phoneys. It had just raced on to the tyre because that was the next thing on its practice-course.

Practice-course?

Yes, because it had been practising on Danielle's obstacles after the park was closed. *That* was why the park keeper had said she could leave them in his compound.

She was absolutely furious. That was so mean! Not even asking! Pretending to give sheepdog-whistles!

She stared at him and his face changed. He had seen her look, and he knew she knew. And he didn't care.

Right, she thought. We'll show him. Won't we, Chuck?

All along she'd told people she didn't mind if Chuck didn't win. All she wanted was for her not to make a fool of herself. And she still didn't mind about winning.

Some other dog could do it faster, fine. Provided it wasn't the park keeper's collie.

She told Chuck to sit, and went over to the man who was beginning to lower the jumps for Chuck, because she was smaller than the collie.

'Can we do the big-dog jumps, please?' she said. 'Chuck loves to jump.'

'If that's how you want it,' said the man, and left them as they were.

Danielle didn't want the park keeper saying afterwards that Chuck beat his collie because she only had titchy little jumps to get over.

Chuck was still sitting, tremble, tremble, tremble.

Danielle went to the first jump.

'Ready?' said the woman who looked after the timer and the scoreboard.

Danielle nodded.

'Five, four, three, two, one, GO!' said the woman.

'OK, Chuck!' cried Danielle. 'Run! Hup!'

Chuck raced to the jump. Ooh, this was a biggie! But if Danielle said . . .

She poised, bunched her haunches beneath her, sprang.

Front feet on bar, back feet on bar, down.

Cheers, but she didn't notice.

Danielle was racing to the ramp.

'Here, Chuck! Run!'

'Five!' yelled the yobs.

Easy up the ramp. Wait in the middle in case it's a tilter. No? Up to the top, then. Down.

Another jump? Can do.

'Ten!' yelled the yobs.

Poise, tense, spring. Over.

What next? Ah – in-and-out-poles.

Chuck skimmed between them as if she were chasing a jinking rabbit.

'Fifteen!'

Another jump. Great. And now?

Up-in-the-air-twisty-thing. Oh, oh. Different. Not Danielle's up-in-the-air-twisty-thing.

'Oh, come on, Chuck. It's all right. It won't bite you. Hup! Good dog. Careful, now. Walk.'

'Twenty!'

Delicately Chuck picked her way along the planks.

'Twenty-five!'

Done it!

Danielle raced to the tyre.

'Run, Chuck! Hup!'

Tyres were tricky. Chuck paused to eye this one.

'Thirty!'

'Hup!'

OK, and she sailed through.

Danielle ran to the seesaw with Chuck at her heels.

'Walk! Careful!'

Easy up. Wait in the middle. Will it? Won't it. Bit more. Ah, there it goes.

'Thirty-five!'

Scuttle down, and . . .

AAAAAARRRRGGGH!

It's a whippet-chomping monster from outer space!

Chuck didn't bolt, quite. But she stopped dead a metre away from the tunnel, crouched, and stared imploringly up at Danielle.

She looked so pathetic that the audience, who'd been cheering her on like crazy – they didn't care for the park keeper either, showing everyone else up like that with his dratted whistle – gave a long, collective sigh of disappointment.

Ooooooooohhh!

'Forty!'

'Oh, come on, Chuck! It's just like the one at home. It's only a tunnel. It won't eat you . . . Oh, Chuck!'

I can't I can't I can't.

Chuck stuck where she was, imploring, tremble, tremble, tremble.

'Forty-five!' yelled the yobs.

Desperately she looked over her shoulder.

And . . .

Jenny and Danielle's mum, and Jason and Rosie and their mum and dad were watching from the far side of the ring. Jason was holding Rosie up so that she could see. Rosie was holding her Obelix balloon. They'd tied a bag of toffees to the end of the string so that if she let go it wouldn't fly away. Jason was jumping up and down, because he's like that, yelling at Chuck to go through the tunnel. Rosie was joggled. She let go of the string. The wind blew the balloon into the ring. The toffees pulled it down. When they touched the ground they stopped pulling so the balloon went up again. It bounced the toffees up off the ground. The wind blew it. The toffees pulled it down. Bounce, bounce, bounce, it floated across the ring.

And Chuck looked over her shoulder and

saw the Obelixmonster bouncing straight at her, horrible, grinning, enormous . . .

Now she bolted.

Straight into the tunnel and out at the other end and over the finishing line.

'Fifty-one!' yelled the yobs.

Danielle used the prize money to buy Chuck a rhinestone collar at one of the stalls.

'And next time the park keeper starts talking about his clever collie,' she said, 'I'll tell him Chuck's not that stupid either. At least she knows when she's got something wrong.'

'You can say that,' said her mum.

But Danielle never got the chance, because nowadays the park keeper is as mean to her as he is to everyone else, and she knows why, and he knows she knows, so mostly he leaves the kids alone when she's around.

And anyway, I doubt if she'd have had the nerve.

Chuck Sees a Ghost

Chuck is psychic.

'It's the only explanation,' Danielle told her mum.

'Flapdoodle,' said her mum, who actually believes in that sort of thing, and doesn't like to make jokes about it.

'What about the feet?' said Danielle.

'That's not psychic, that's crazy,' said her mum.

The feet?

Danielle and her mum live in what's called a half-basement. To get to their front door you come down some narrow steps to a little front yard, where the dustbins are.

Danielle's bedroom window faces the street. If she gets right up close she can see the passers-by, but when she's in bed all she can see is their legs.

Chuck sleeps on Danielle's bed, curled up against her back. They have the curtains open because Chuck is afraid of the dark and there's a bit of light from the streetlamps.

(This is what Danielle says. As a matter of fact she used to sleep with the curtains open *before* she got Chuck, for some reason.)

Early in the morning, feet start going past. Danielle's so used to them that she sleeps right through. So does Chuck, mostly.

But . . .

Sometimes the feet are DANGEROUS!

The first Danielle knows about it is that something has biffed her, hard, in the middle of her back, Chuck isn't there any more, and there's the sound of feet walking away along the pavement.

(The biff was Chuck springing off the bed.)

'Stupid dog,' mutters Danielle.

It's not just maddening – it's double-maddening. It's maddening because it wakes her up, and it's double-maddening because then she lies awake trying to figure out what made that particular lot of feet dangerous.

She can hear them going away down the street, so she knows it isn't always the same feet. It might be a man with nails in his boots, or a jogger, or a woman in heels, or someone with a squeaky sole – anything.

Then, when she's just about given up figuring and is starting to drop off again, Chuck comes out from under the bed where she's been hiding, and hops up and licks her ear to make sure she's still alive, and then wakes her up some more by going round and round and round until she's sure she's got exactly the right place to lie down, and goes straight off to sleep as if nothing had happened.

And then some more feet come by and Chuck doesn't even stir, and Danielle lies awake trying to figure out about that.

Double-

Triple-

Quadruple-maddening!

'They must be vampires going home from a hard night's bloodsucking,' she said.

'Flapdoodle,' said her mum.

Chuck also sees ghosts.

Or something.

She'll be walking along, sniffing a bit here and there, peering into gateways in case of lurking Monstercats, nothing special.

And then her ears will go right up and she'll get into her prancy, tiptoe walk and stare ahead down the pavement when there isn't anything there at all that Danielle can see, not even a leaf being twirled around in the wind.

She'll go past several gateways like that, not bothering about Monstercats, and then the ghost will disappear (supposing things *can* disappear when they're already invisible) and she'll go back to sniffing and peering into gateways as if nothing had happened.

Mostly the whatever-it-is seems to be straight ahead, along the pavement, but sometimes it's moving and Chuck's head turns slowly as she watches it cross the road. Once one came along the middle of the road and Chuck watched it go past, twisting her neck right round to follow it while she was still walking straight ahead. She looked weird like that.

'I think it's got to be ghosts of rabbits,' said Danielle. 'You keep saying all this used to be countryside round here.'

'Chuck's never seen a rabbit,' said her mum.

'Deer too,' said Danielle. 'That one last week was sort of up in the air, and it was really moving. Fast, I mean. And do you remember when she hid under the milk-float? I bet you that was a bear.'

'There haven't been wild bears in England for thousands of years,' said her mum.

'Yes there have,' said Danielle. 'We did it in school. I don't remember when, but there were. Or it was a wolf. You'll give me wolves, won't you?'

'Flapdoodle,' said her mum.

Jenny was more sympathetic about Chuck being psychic.

'Do you think she could tell our fortunes?' she said.

'Difficult,' said Danielle. 'I mean she might *know* our fortunes, but how's she going to tell us!'

'She's got to point to things,' said Jenny. 'Things belonging to different people. You put them out in a circle and put Chuck in the middle and . . . I know – socks!'

'Socks?' said Danielle.

'We get Harriet and Howard and Jason and the others to bring one of their socks up to the park, before it's been to the wash of course because it'll be good and smelly and she'll like that, and then we put them round and ask her things like who's going to get married first and see whose sock she chooses.'

So they got some of their friends together and went up to the park. Everybody brought a dirty sock. Danielle tied Chuck's lead to a small tree, loose, so that it could slip round, and they laid the socks out in a circle so she could just reach them and started to ask her questions.

It was all too much for Chuck. She knew Danielle wanted her to do something but she couldn't figure what, and it was all her fault because it always is.

And everyone was trying to coax her into going and choosing a sock, but joshing around at the same time, which made it worse.

All she wanted to do was creep towards Danielle, grovel, grovel, grovel, please, please forgive me for the awful thing I've done whatever it was, tremble, tremble, tremble.

Danielle was just about to tell everyone to stop when a huge black dog – he still looked like a puppy but he was enormous – came prancing up and joined in.

He was playing a different game, though. He took one of the socks and ran off with it.

'Hey! That's my dad's!' yelled Jason.

(He'd stolen it out of the wash because he knew it would be *really* smelly. He's like that.)

They all dashed off after the black dog, who pranced around for a bit playing hard-to-get, and then dropped Jason's dad's sock and came galloping back for one of the others and dashed off with that.

It did this several times until someone had the sense to pick up the rest of the socks, and then it decided that the game was over and ran off with the one it was carrying, which was Harriet's. Harriet likes to wear odd socks, on purpose, so she said she didn't mind and no-one would notice.

'That wasn't really a dog,' said Danielle afterwards.

'It was enough of a dog for me, thank you,' said Jenny.

'Didn't you notice Chuck?' said Danielle. 'You remember how miz she'd got? And she doesn't usually like big floppy dogs – I have to pick her up and carry her. But as soon as this one showed up, she forgot about being miz and was really interested. She sat and watched him fooling around and even when he came charging towards her she wasn't bothered.'

'So?' said Jenny.

'*And* he hadn't got a collar,' said Danielle.

'You're telling me Chuck isn't scared of big floppy dogs provided they haven't got collars?' said Jenny. 'Except it wasn't a dog, anyway? And I have two heads?'

'He was an other-world protector,' said Danielle.

'Make that three heads,' said Jenny.

'You know I keep saying you could get Chuck's brain in a thimble?' said Danielle. 'Well, you couldn't. It's as big as an egg, really. Almost, I mean. And she's got to be doing something with it, hasn't she? I think she's being psychic with it. She's got this other-world to figure out, where the ghosts come from and the feet belong, so she's only got a thimbleful to spare for thinking about this world.'

'If you say so,' said Jenny.

'And I don't think the other-world likes us fooling around with it, as if it was only a game,' said Danielle. 'So it sent that dog to break it up and look after Chuck. That's why Chuck knew the dog was OK. See?'

She didn't really believe this, of course, but it was a neat idea, and it meant she could stop the others trying anything like the sock game with Chuck again.

But she did really sort of half-think that Chuck might be a bit fey, and she *was* seeing something in the street, and there *was* something different about the feet, maybe.

Still, she wasn't prepared for what happened with the man with the van with the yellow donkey on it.

She was sitting on a bench just inside the park gate, waiting for Jenny and reading a story about a dragon-slaying princess. Chuck was curled up on the grass, watching the people going in and out.

The princess was just meeting her first *REALLY BIG* dragon, so Danielle wasn't noticing anything much until Chuck suddenly jerked herself on to her feet.

She stared. Her ears pricked up. Her eyes glistened. The hair between her shoulders stood up stiff as a toothbrush. Danielle had never seen that happen before, so she knew this one had to be a truly weird ghost. Chuck's ghosts were invisible, of course, but Danielle couldn't help looking to see what she was staring at.

Nothing.

Well, there was this bloke getting out of a battered old van, middling size, bright blue with a yellow donkey painted on the side. Chuck's eyes followed him as he walked into the park, so Danielle knew it had to be something to do with him.

He was wearing faded blue jeans and a grubby Pink Floyd T-shirt, and small brass-rimmed specs, and a blue denim cap back to front. He had a pencil tucked behind his ear. He had a brown, outdoor

face and straggly blond hair and a beard.

He walked into the park with a loose, easy stride, dropped a plastic carrier bag into the litter-bin opposite Danielle's bench, and went back to the van.

Chuck watched him the whole way.

There was a woman in the passenger seat of the van but Danielle couldn't see her very well.

They drove off, and Chuck lay down as if nothing had happened at all.

It was so weird that she couldn't help telling her

mum about it, although she knew she wouldn't be interested.

'Honestly,' she said, 'it was just this bloke. There was this old blue van with a yellow donkey on it and this bloke got out and came and put a bag of rubbish in the bin, and Chuck stared at him as if he'd been the ghostiest ghost she'd ever seen.'

'What did he look like?' said her mum.

'Just ordinary,' said Danielle. 'Like an old-fashioned hippy, I suppose. A bit grubby. One of those old rock groups on his T-shirt. And a beard and straggly hair. Oh, yes, and funny little specs . . .'

She was spreading butter on her toast while she talked, so she wasn't watching her mum, who'd got up to get another block of butter out of the fridge as Danielle had taken the last. Now, a bit like feeling a draught under the door, she sensed that something in the room had changed.

She looked up. Her mum was standing by the fridge with the butter in her hand and the door still open, staring out at the garden as if she'd seen a ghost too.

'What's up?' said Danielle. 'Are you all right, Mum?'

'Go on,' said her mum. 'This man. Did he look at you? Did he say anything?'

'He didn't even notice me,' said Danielle. 'Oh, I don't think he was one of those. Honestly. You needn't worry. Let's talk about something else.'

'He had a pencil behind his ear, didn't he?' said her mum.

'I forgot . . . You mean you know him? That's amazing! Chuck really is psychic! You've got to . . .'

She stopped. She shouldn't have started. Joking about Chuck's ghosts wasn't a good idea. Her mum was obviously upset.

Her mum closed the fridge, got a plate out of the cupboard, unwrapped the butter slowly and put it on the plate.

'That was your father,' she said.

Danielle didn't say anything. She felt her stomach go small.

'I lived in that van for five years, until you came along,' said her mum. 'Do you want me to tell you about him?'

'It doesn't have to be now,' said Danielle.

'Might as well,' said her mum. 'I've been putting it off, but . . . Oh, hell. Let's get it over.'

The next bit is private. It took about half an hour. After a bit Danielle picked Chuck up and put her on her lap, for something to hold, and she lay there, not even trembling, as if nothing was wrong at all. It might have been, once, but it wasn't any longer.

'. . . so I knew it was time to quit,' said Danielle's mum. 'Like I've said, he's not a bad guy, very easy to get along with, only hopeless. He's not a bad artist – that's why he carries the pencil – but he's never going to bother to get any better. I could cope so long as it was just us, but after you were born and I realized he still wasn't going to take any responsibility . . . not for anything, ever . . . I'm sorry . . . Do you want to talk to him? I think I could get in touch. I still know one or two people . . .'

Danielle shook her head.

'He didn't look as if he'd be very interested,' she said.

'I'm afraid not,' said her mum. 'That's one of the things that made it so hard telling you. I didn't know if you'd believe me. And I really didn't want you to be hurt.'

Danielle thought about it.

'It's all right,' she said. 'It's made a real difference, actually seeing him. I felt as if there was a sort of hole in me, not knowing, and now perhaps there isn't any more.'

'It was difficult for me, too,' said her mum. 'Five years of my life . . . gone . . .'

She looked up and gave her head a little shake and smiled.

'Don't worry, darling. I wouldn't go back for the whole world. As far as I'm concerned, you're the best thing that ever happened to me.'

Danielle slipped across and sat in her lap and hugged her, and Chuck, who understands about laps, hopped up too and licked their faces because they were there.

'You're right about her,' said Danielle's mum. 'She really is psychic.'

'Flapdoodle,' said Danielle.

'Well, that's over,' said her mum. 'Let's go and celebrate. What would you like to do?'

Danielle had an idea. It was a bit like the one she'd had about not having to leave the flat because of the hard rock, but this time she couldn't quite make it work. Ah well, she thought. Give it a go.

'You really wouldn't go back for the whole world?' she said.

'No,' said her mum.

'The whole universe?' said Danielle. 'Because if Chuck hadn't seen that ghost . . .'

'There's a gap in your logic,' said her mum.

Then she laughed.

'Never mind,' she said. 'Perhaps she's saved *our* universe. Where's the nearest McDonald's?'

THE END

ABOUT THE AUTHOR

PETER DICKINSON was born in 1927, in Zambia. At his first school, baboons used to raid the tangerine tree in the playground, and the local swimming pool was a big wooden cage let down into the Zambezi river – to keep the crocodiles out. He came back to England when he was seven. He has written a lot of books, some of which have won prizes. He has four children and several grandchildren, and lives in Hampshire with his second wife, the American writer Robin McKinley, and their three whippets, Rowan, Holly and Hazel (a.k.a. 'Chuck').

ABOUT CHUCK

Peter says, 'When Robin came to England to marry me, she brought Rowan with her. Rowan is white with brindle blotches, and a bit broody. She hated to be left alone so, in America, Robin took her everywhere with her. We didn't want to have to do that in England, so we got Holly and Hazel to keep her company. Holly is brown all over, an eager, fidgety clown. Her parents were found wandering and someone took care of them, so we don't know anything about her pedigree. She's just a whippet-shaped dog. Hazel has a huge pedigree, full of champions, but she's far too small to show, so we could buy her as a pet. She's just like she is in the book. I haven't made any of that up. We call her Chuck when we don't want her to guess we're talking about her. (We call the other two Pooh and Bill.)

In the book, Chuck needed an owner, so I made Danielle up, and her mum and Jenny and the others. But Chuck is real.'

HARRIET'S HARE

by Dick King-Smith

All of a sudden, the hare said, loudly and clearly, 'Good morning.'

Hares don't talk. Everyone knows that. But the hare Harriet meets one morning in a corn circle in her father's wheatfield is a very unusual hare: a visitor from the far-off planet Pars, come to spend his holidays on Earth in the form of a talking hare. Wiz, as Harriet names her magical new friend, can speak any language, transform himself into any shape – and, as the summer draws to its close, he has one last, lovely surprise in store for Harriet . . .

WINNER OF THE 1995 CHILDREN'S BOOK AWARD

'Weaves fantasy and reality in a beguiling novel . . . a throughly satisfying read' *Books for Your Children*

'A tale well told' *The School Librarian*

Illustrated by Valerie Littlewood

0 440 86340 6

POOR BADGER

by K.M. Peyton

'I must go and see Badger! He needs me . . .'

Ros falls instantly in love with the beautiful black-and-white pony that she discovers tethered in a field near her home. She has always longed for a pony of her own. If only he belonged to her . . .

But Badger (as Ros and her friend, Leo, name the pony) belongs to someone else, and Ros watches with mounting horror as she sees the way his real owners treat him. At first it is just neglect, but worse is to come and, as the long cold winter nights draw in, Ros knows that she can no longer bear to stand by and see the once-beautiful pony suffer. Together with Leo, she hatches a desperate plan – a plan to rescue poor Badger. . .

A heart-warming and dramatic tale from award-winning author K.M. Peyton

0 440 862655